JET SET
T-REX

CHRISTOPHER QUIRK   **ELEONORA CALI'**

Want more **FREE BOOKS** by *Christopher Quirk.* Visit
www.thealexanderbooks.com

A dinosaur's
favourite
thing to do
Other than
trample
and roar
Is to travel
and see
the world
On a jet set
worldwide
tour

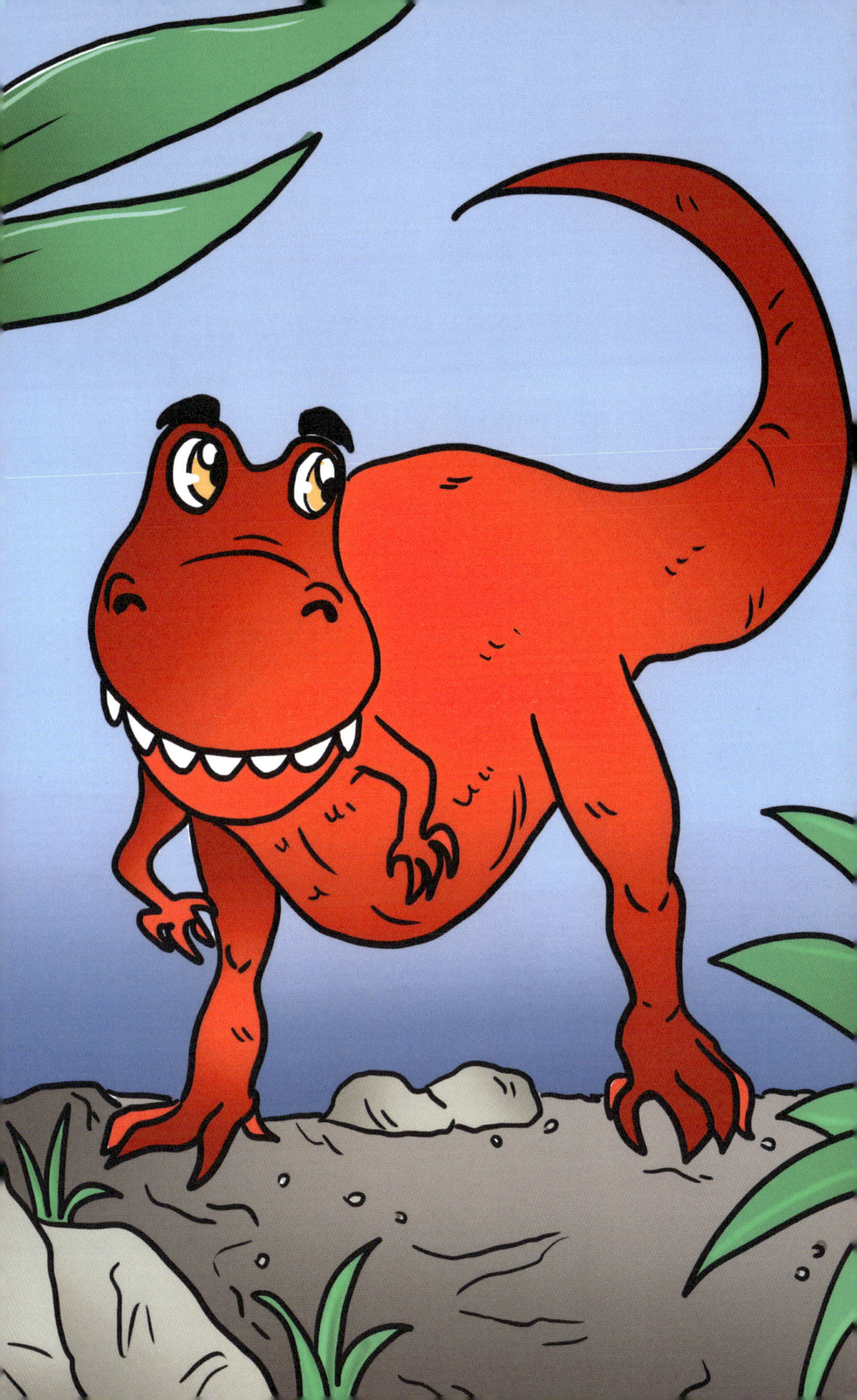

He stomped
over to
the airport
Then boarded
plane
number three
And sat
down between
a family
In seat
number
23B

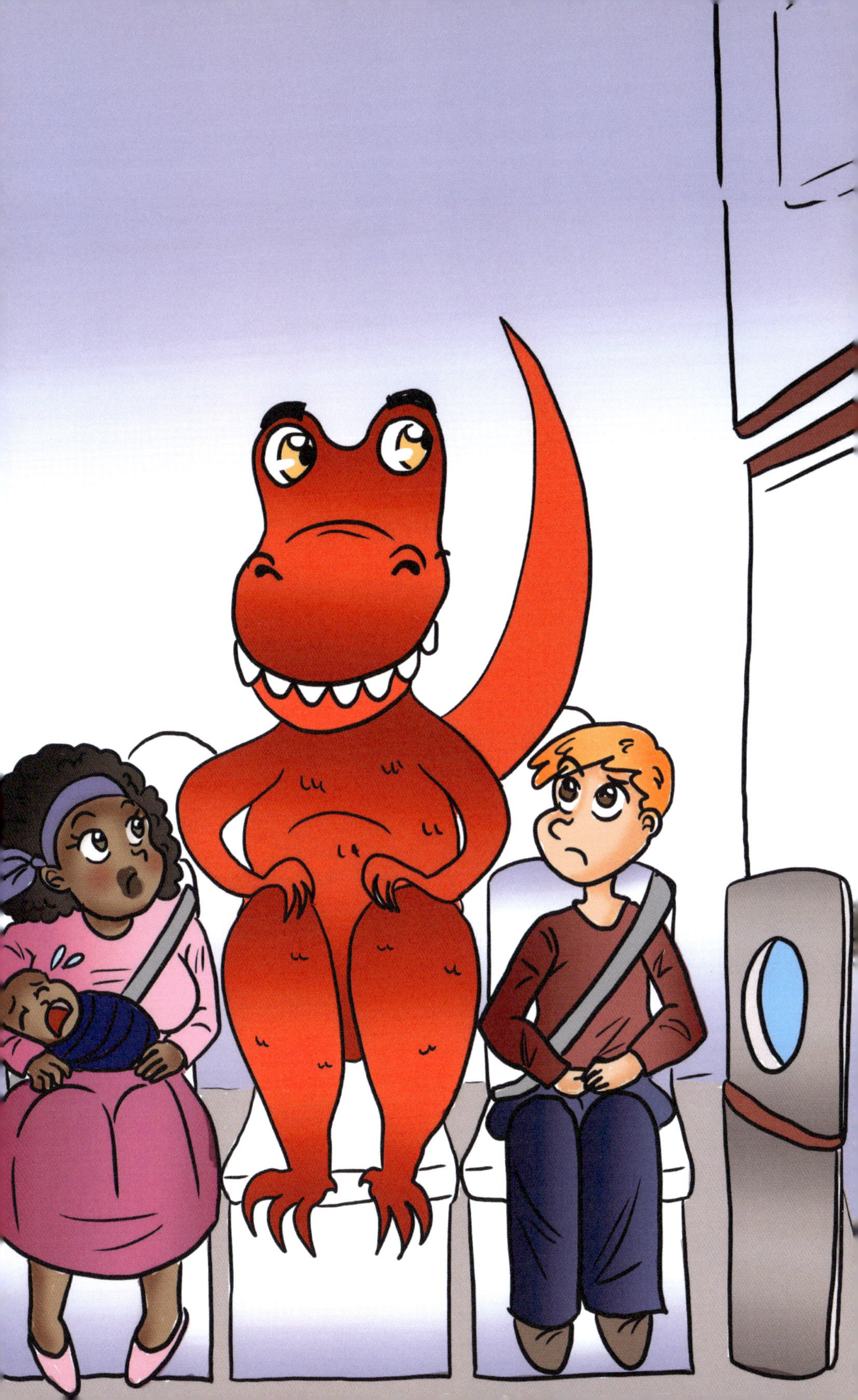

The plane
flew
into Paris
So T-Rex
could see
the Louvre
He met a
famous
artist
Who asked
him not
to move

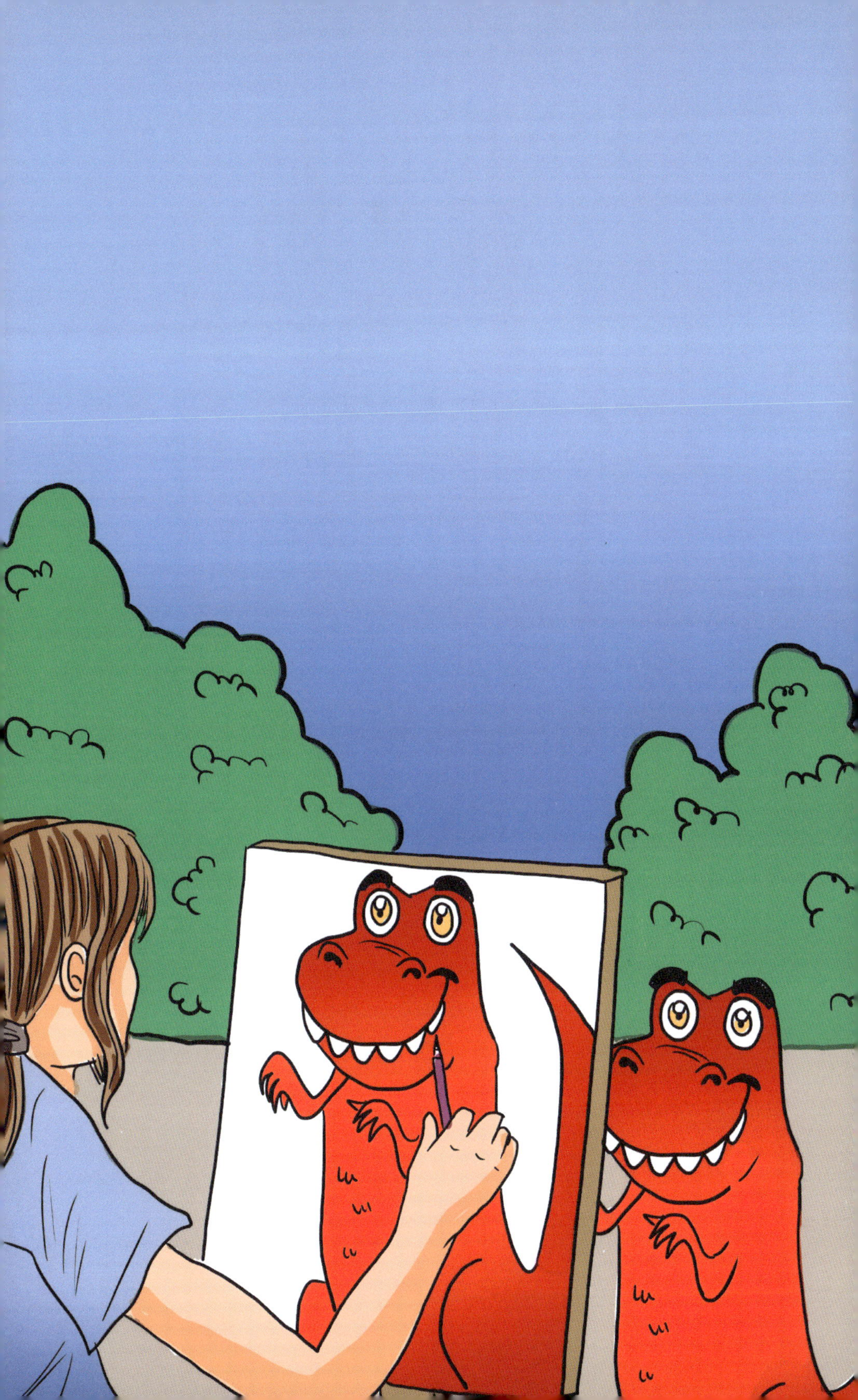

His portrait
went in
the gallery
You couldn't
tell them
apart
And just
like that T-Rex
became
A dinosaur
work of
art

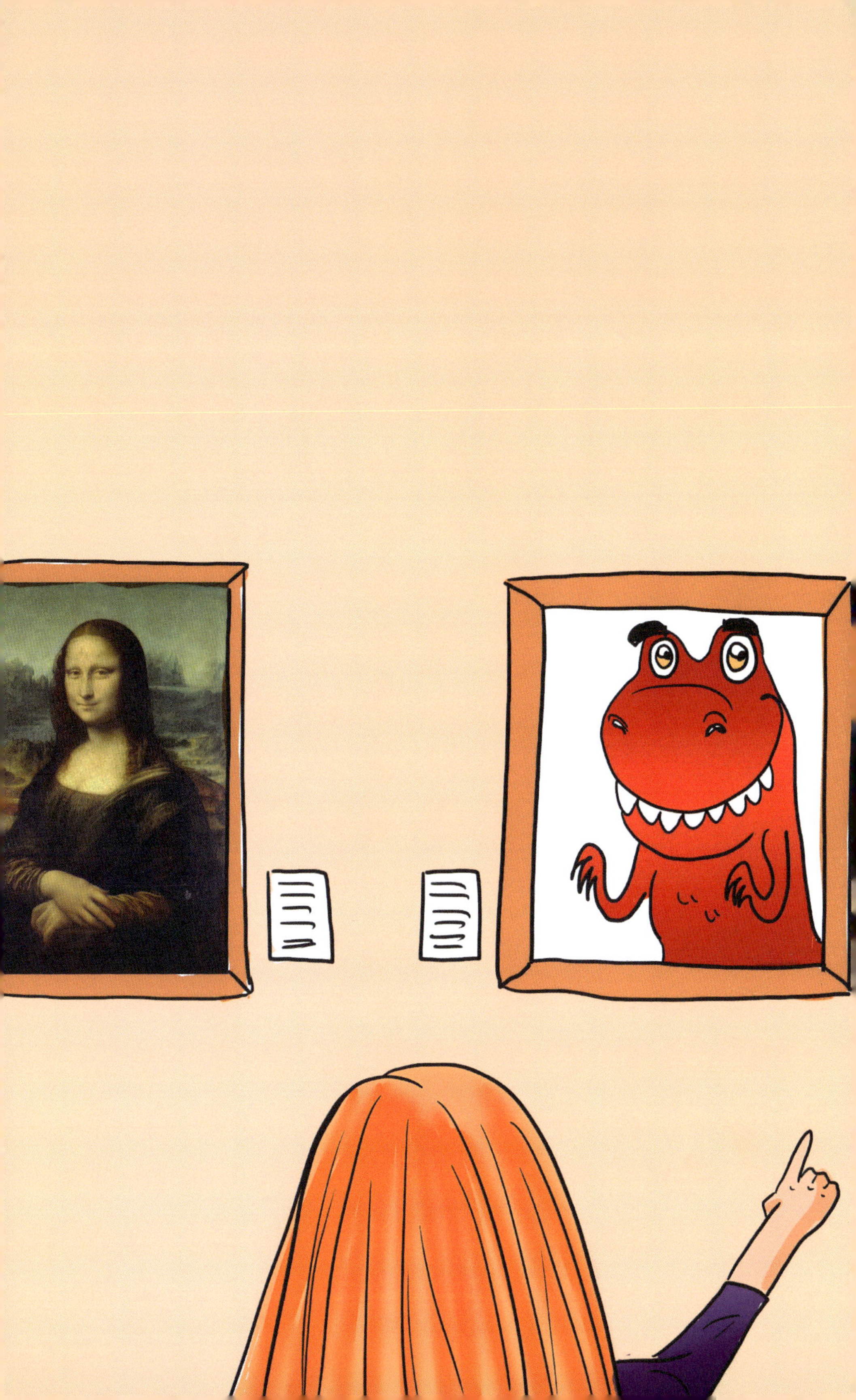

He travelled
down to
Africa
To see the
watering
hole
Rehoming
a herd of
zebras
Was jet set
T-Rex's
goal

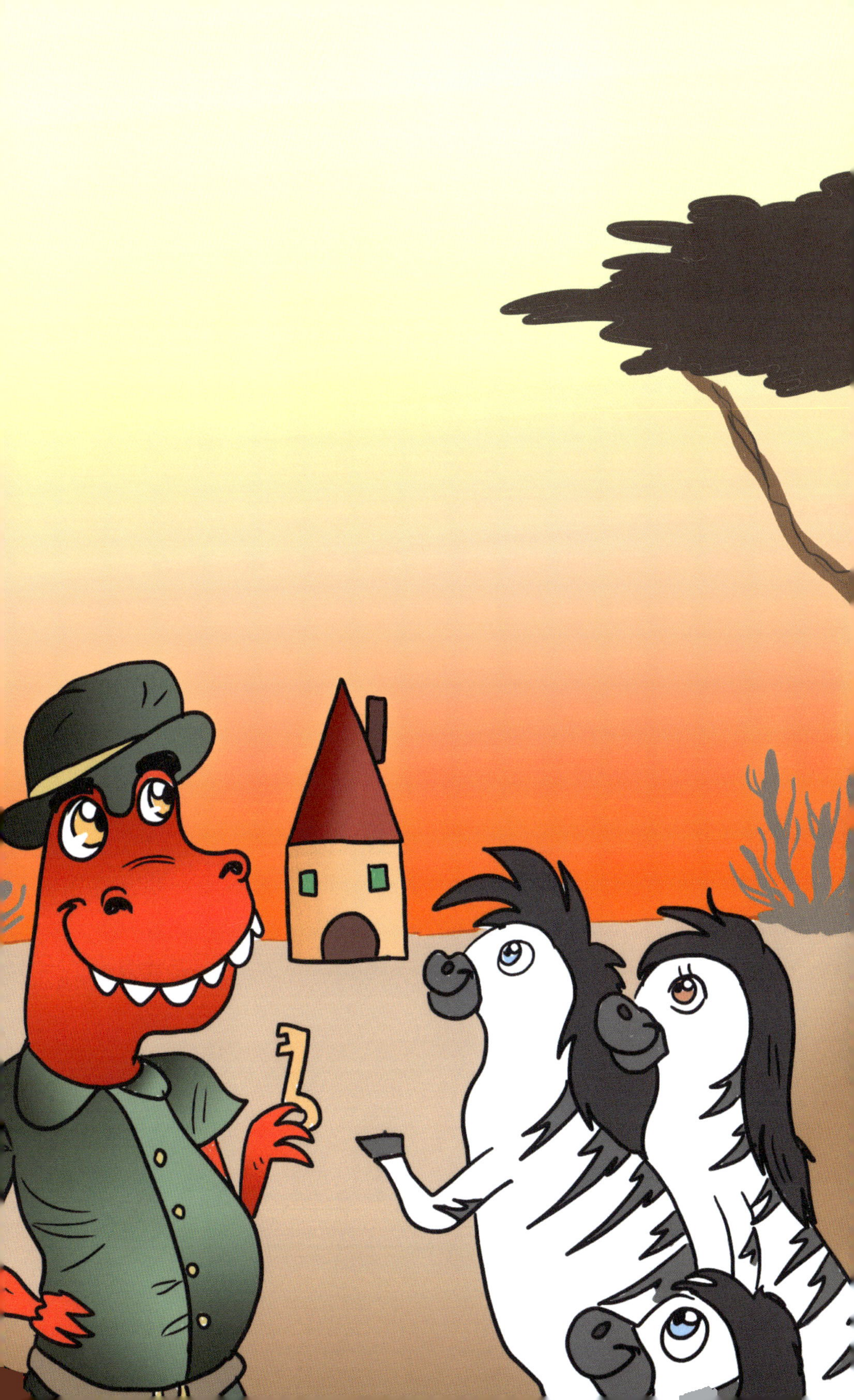

A lion
approached
the T-Rex
And knelt
down
in a bow
Congratulations
jet set
T-Rex
The king
of the jungle
now!

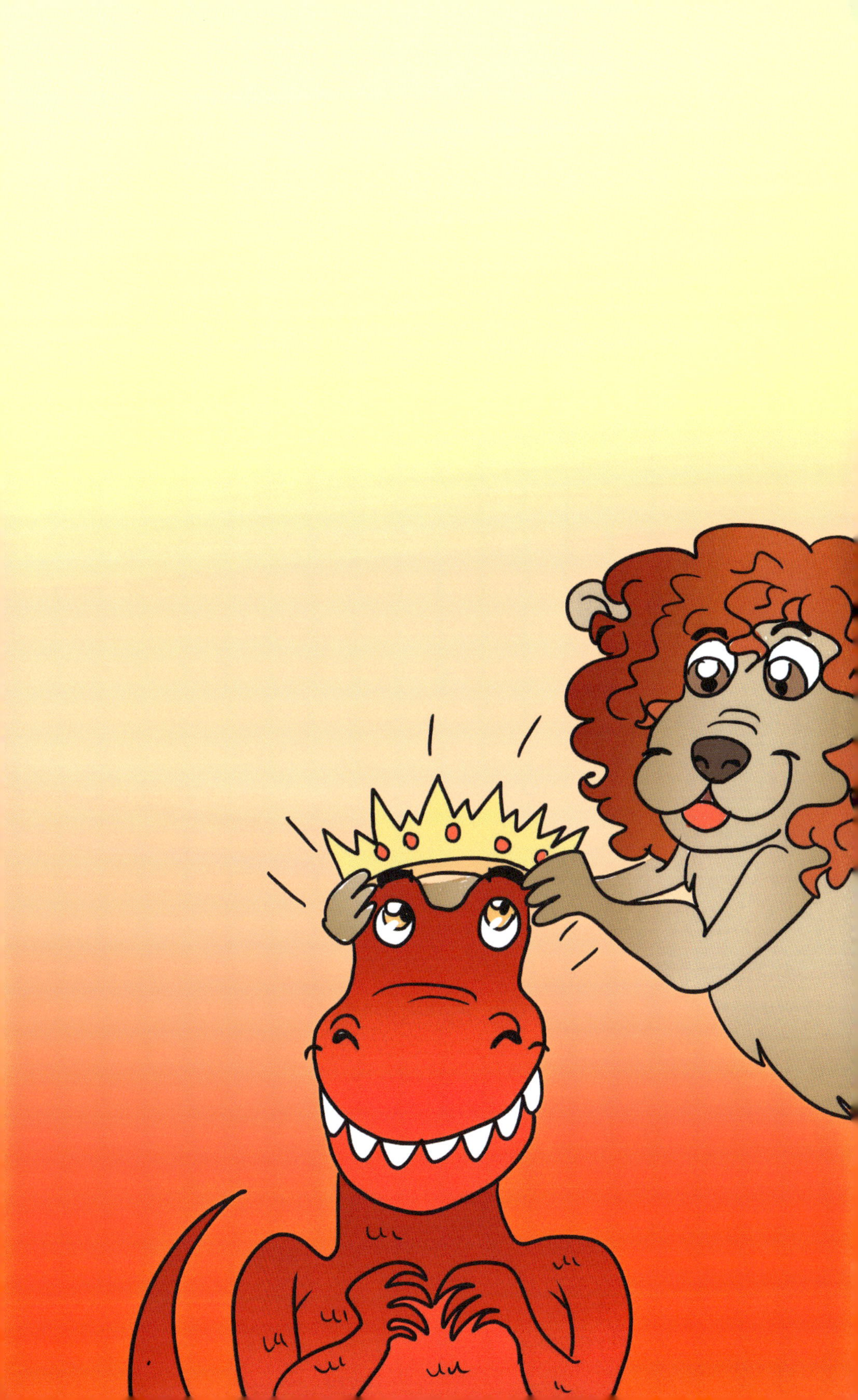

He hopped
on a plane
to Russia
Where
buildings were
really old
He had
to put his
gloves on
So he
couldn't feel
the cold

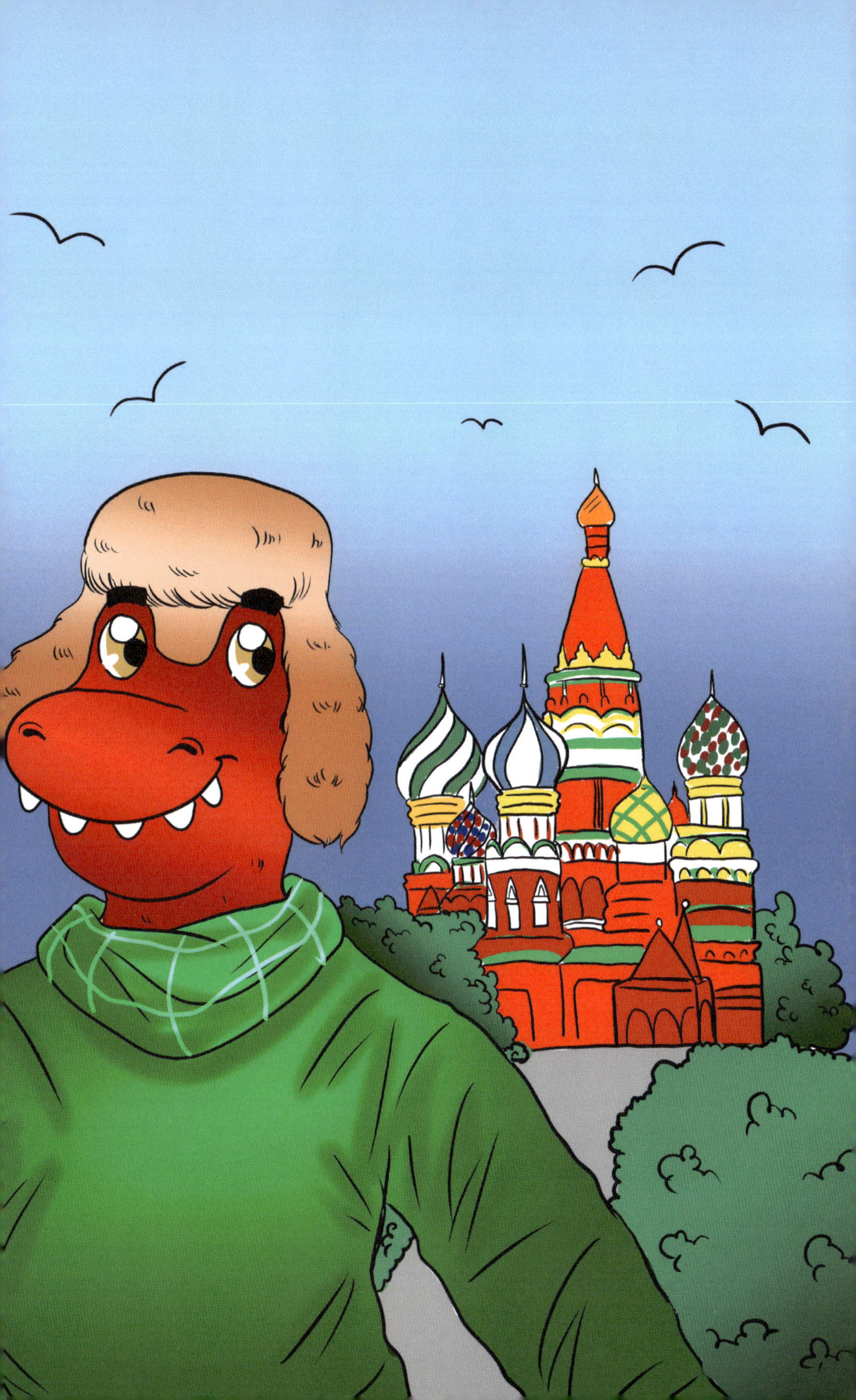

First,
　　he put on
　　　　　a jumper
Then had
　　to put on
　　　　them all
Just like
　　that the
　　　　T-Rex was
A dinosaur
　　Russian
　　　　doll

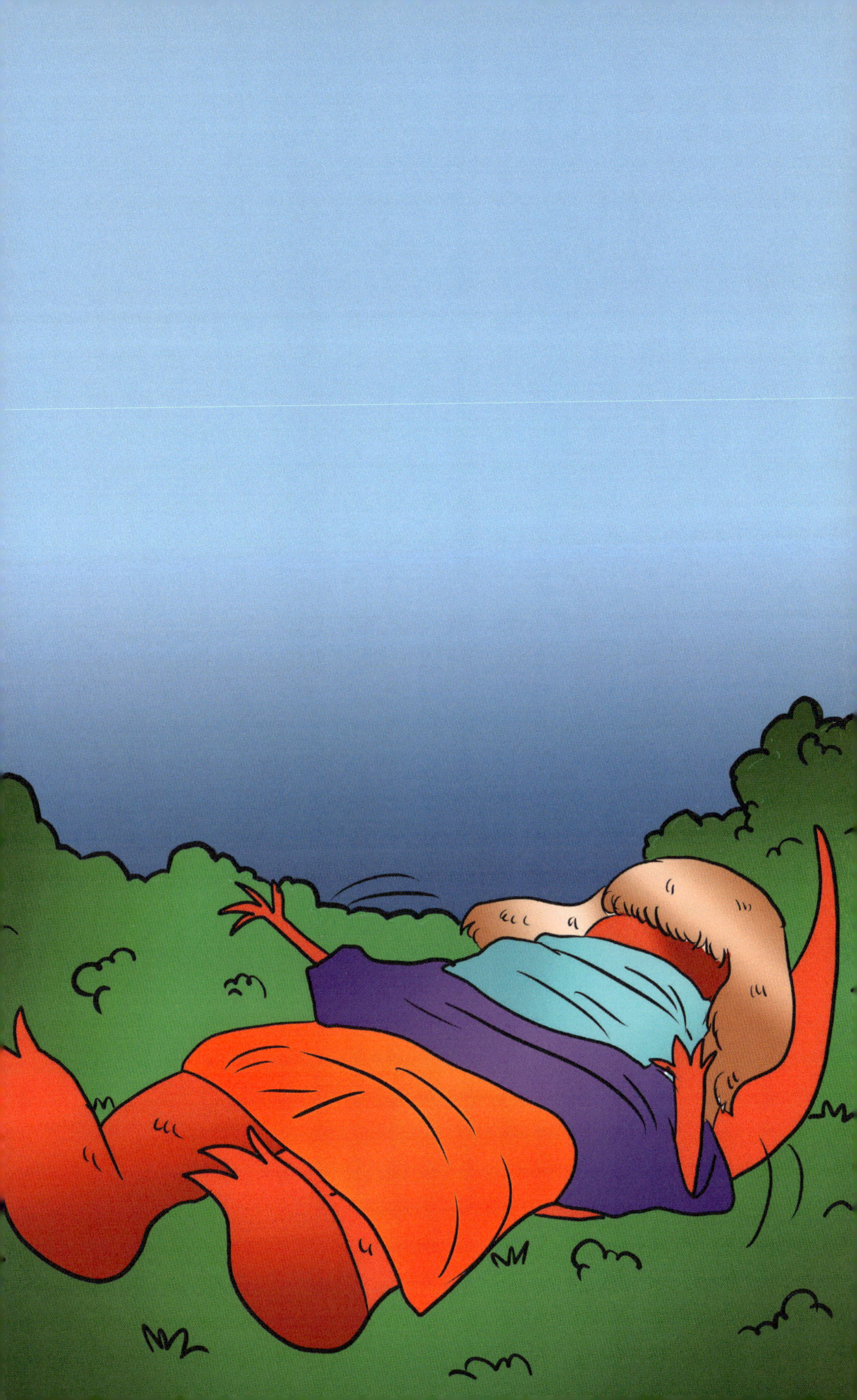

He then
flew across
to India
To see
the
Taj Mahal
He ate
bucket loads
of street food
Chapatis,
Tandoori
and Dhal

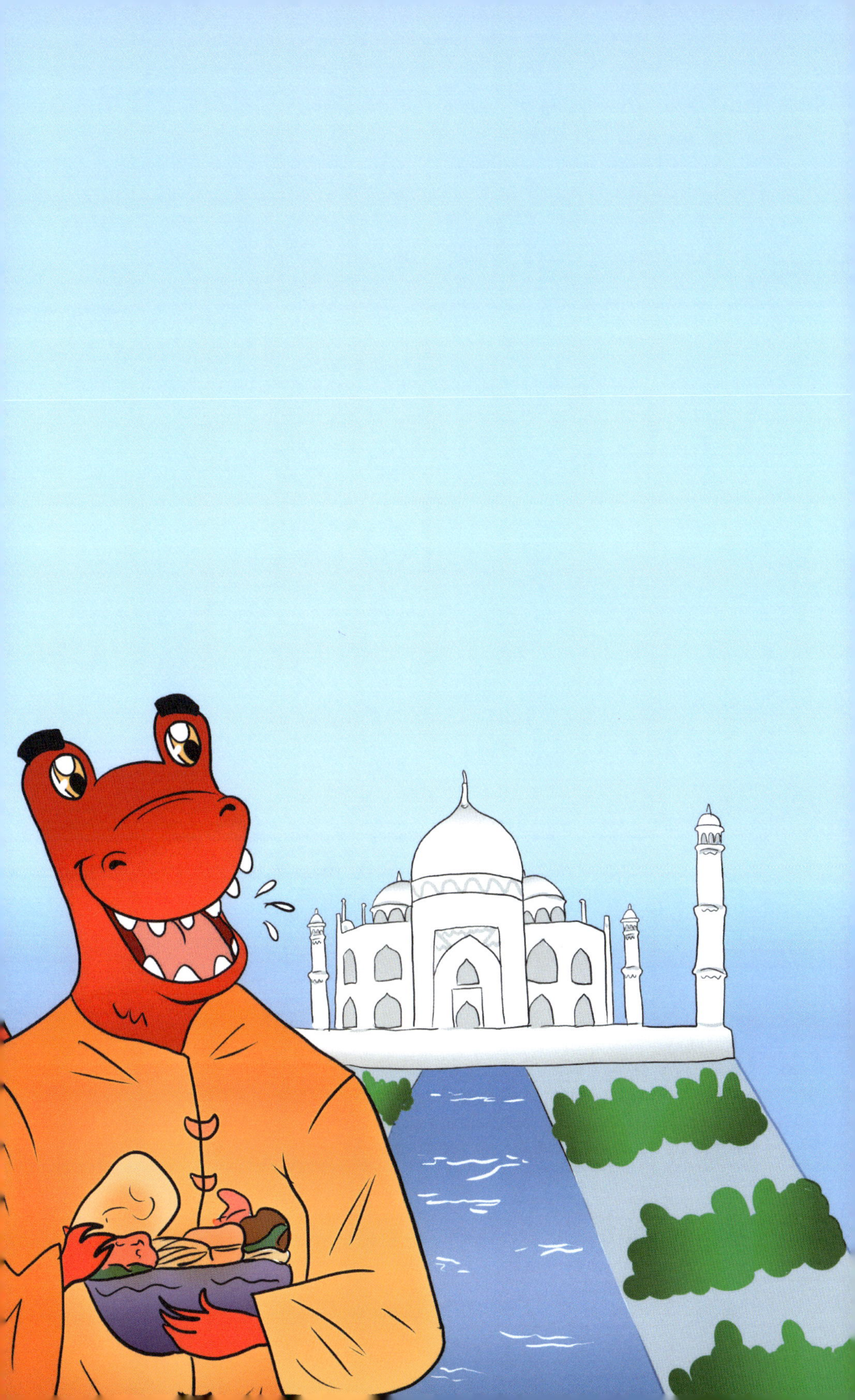

He saw
the Holi
festival
With oranges,
yellows
and blues
Colours
enjoyed
by everyone
Dinosaurs,
me
and you

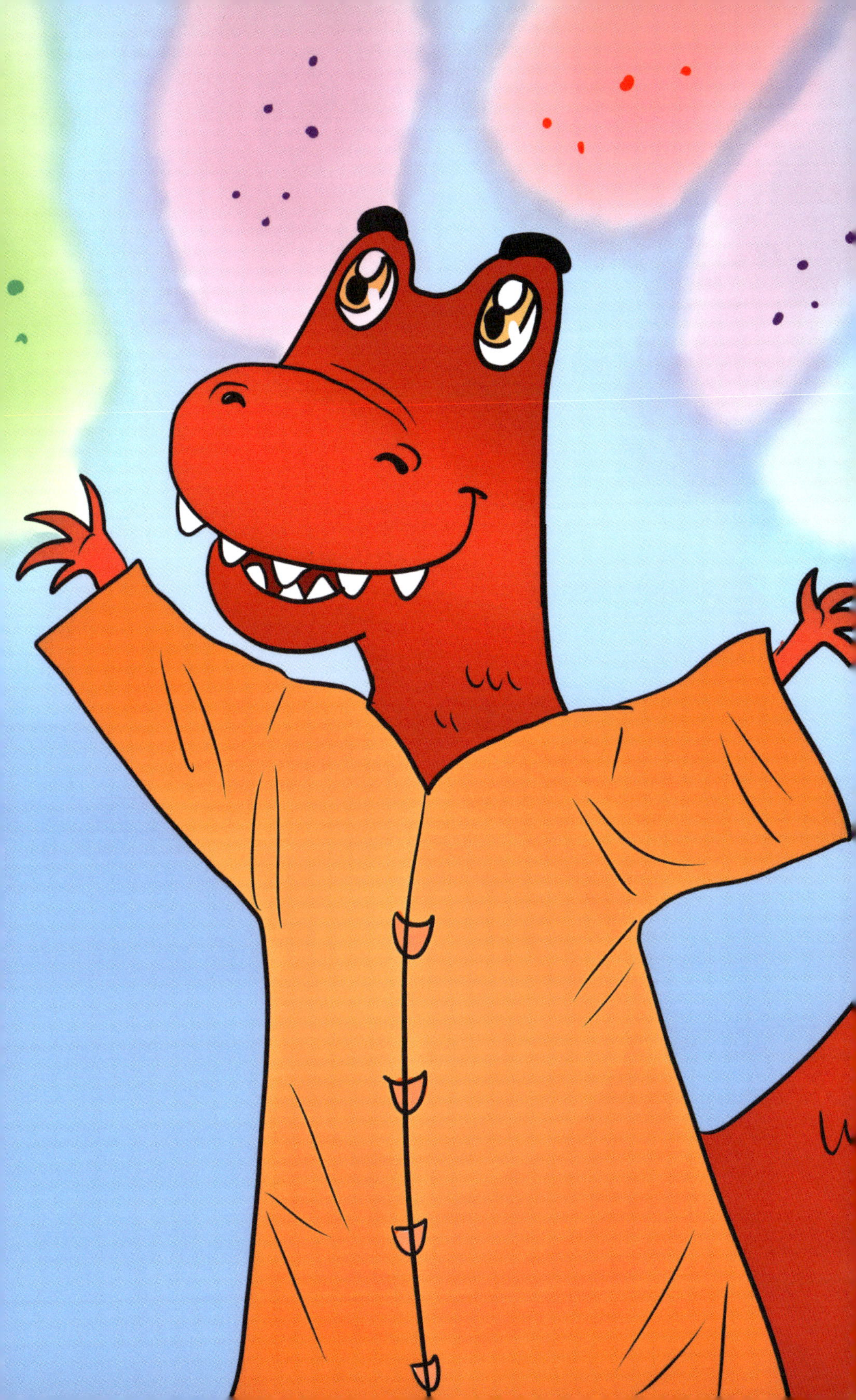

He got on
a plane
to China
And gave
Panda
a call
They went
to see the
temples
And then
visit the
Great Wall

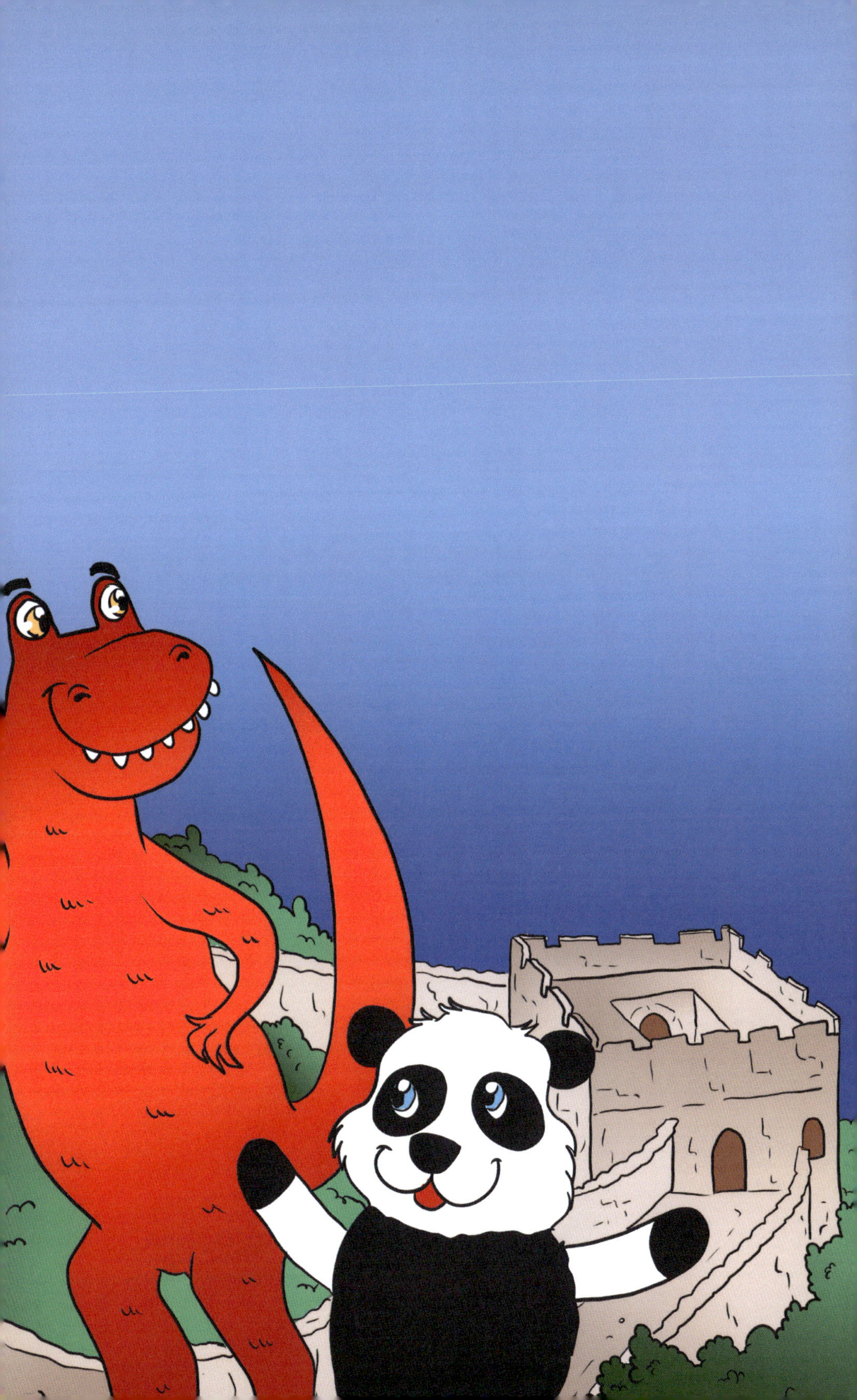

He learnt
how to do
martial arts
And break
boards with
his hand
T-Rex the
kung fu
grand master
The best
in all the
land

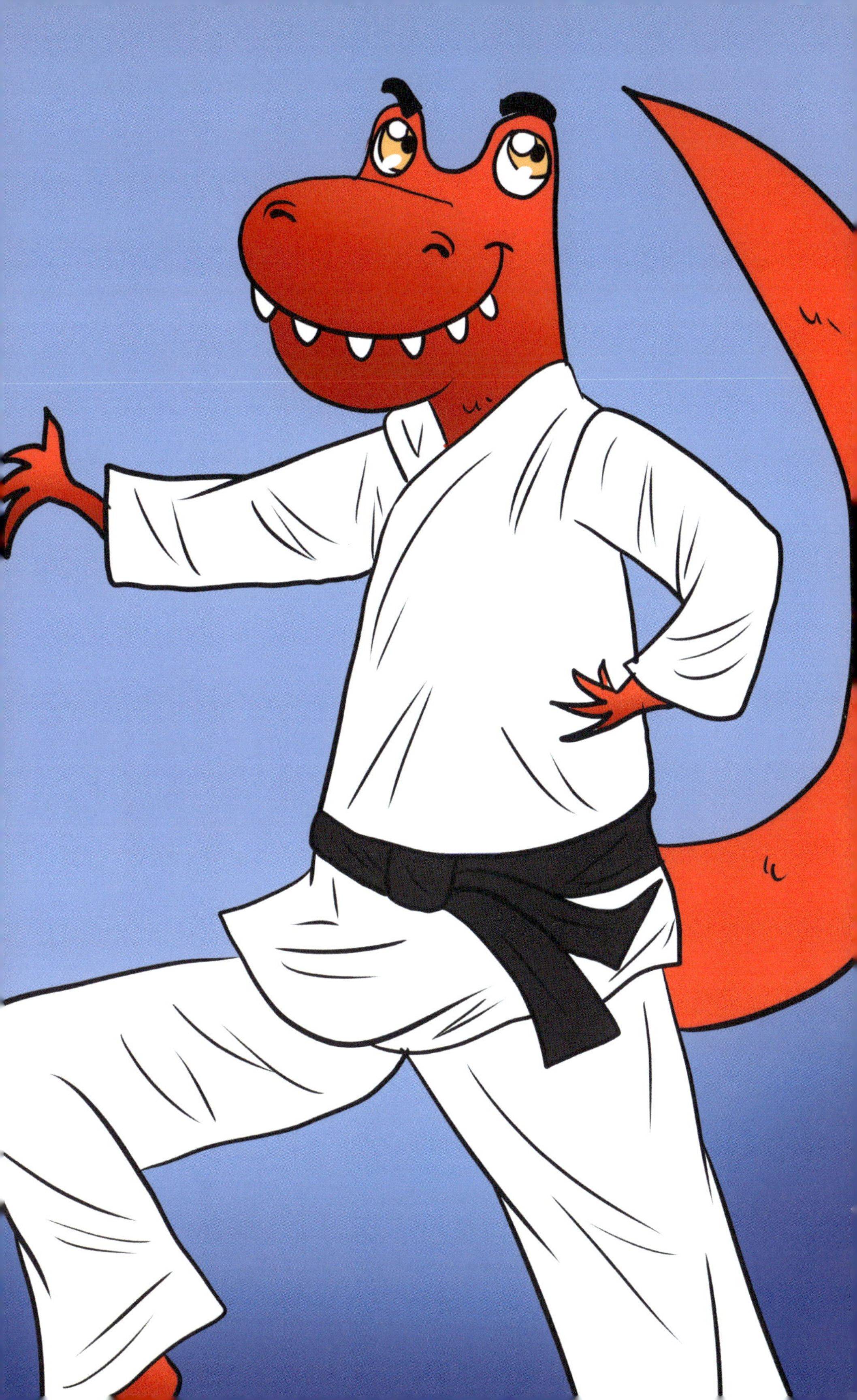

He made

it to Sydney

Harbour

And met

with a

kangaroo

To show him

how to sing

and dance

Over a BBQ

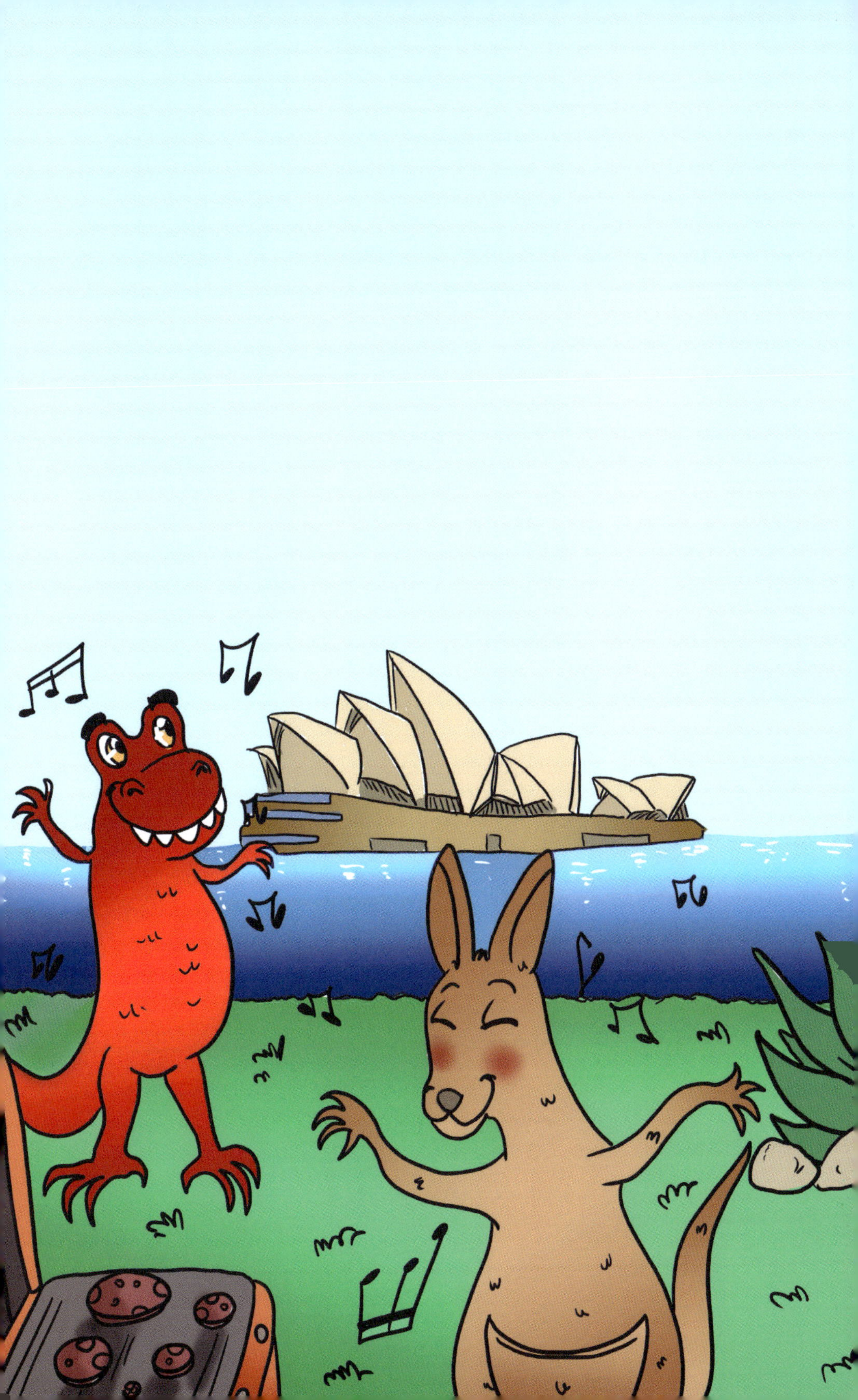

Then all at once he was
on stage
Tapping a beat with
his toe
Tonight, at the Sydney
Opera House
The dinosaur one-man
show

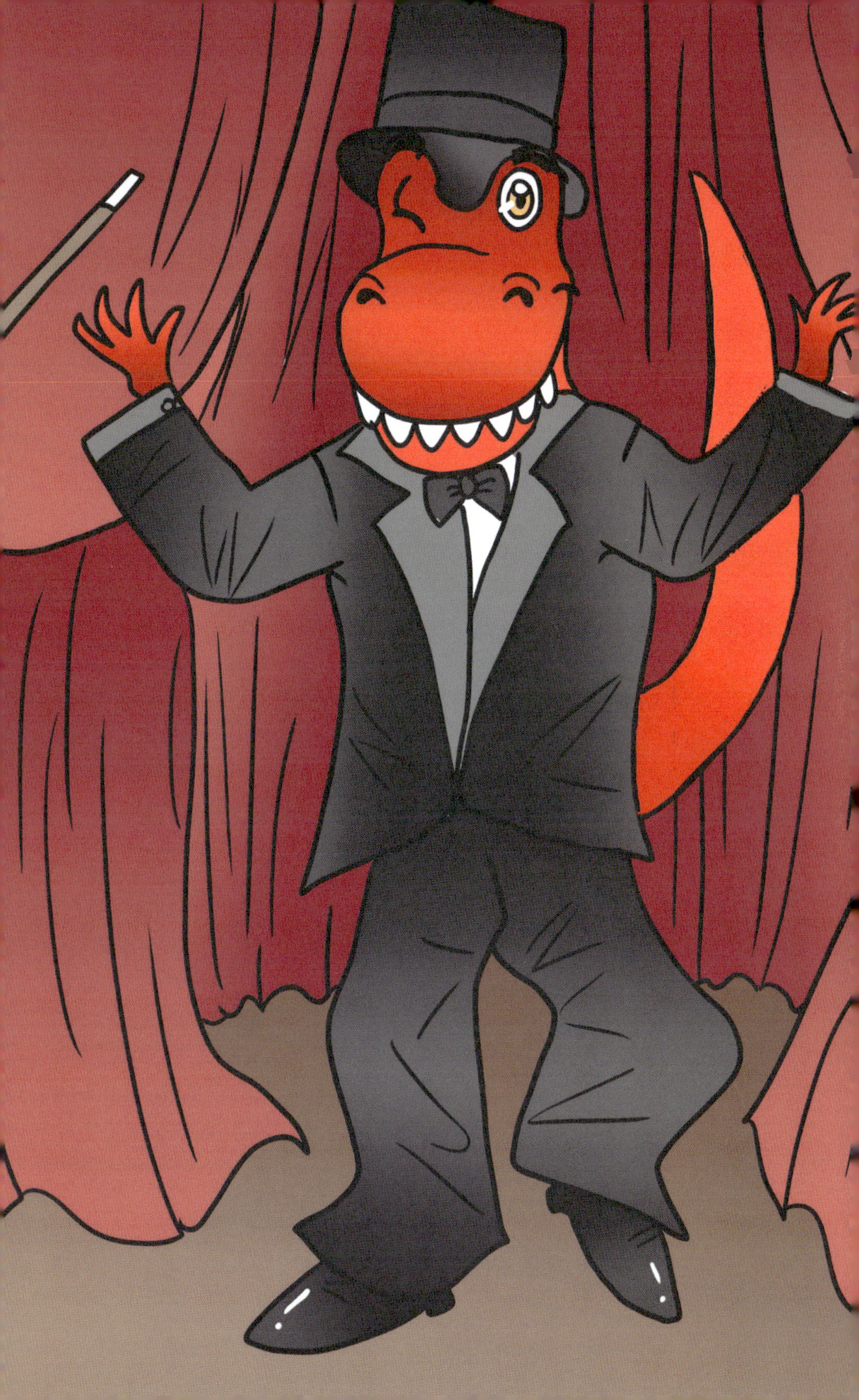

He got on
a plane to
Antarctica
To dance
upon
the ice
He was joined
by bears
and foxes
And even
Antarctic
mice

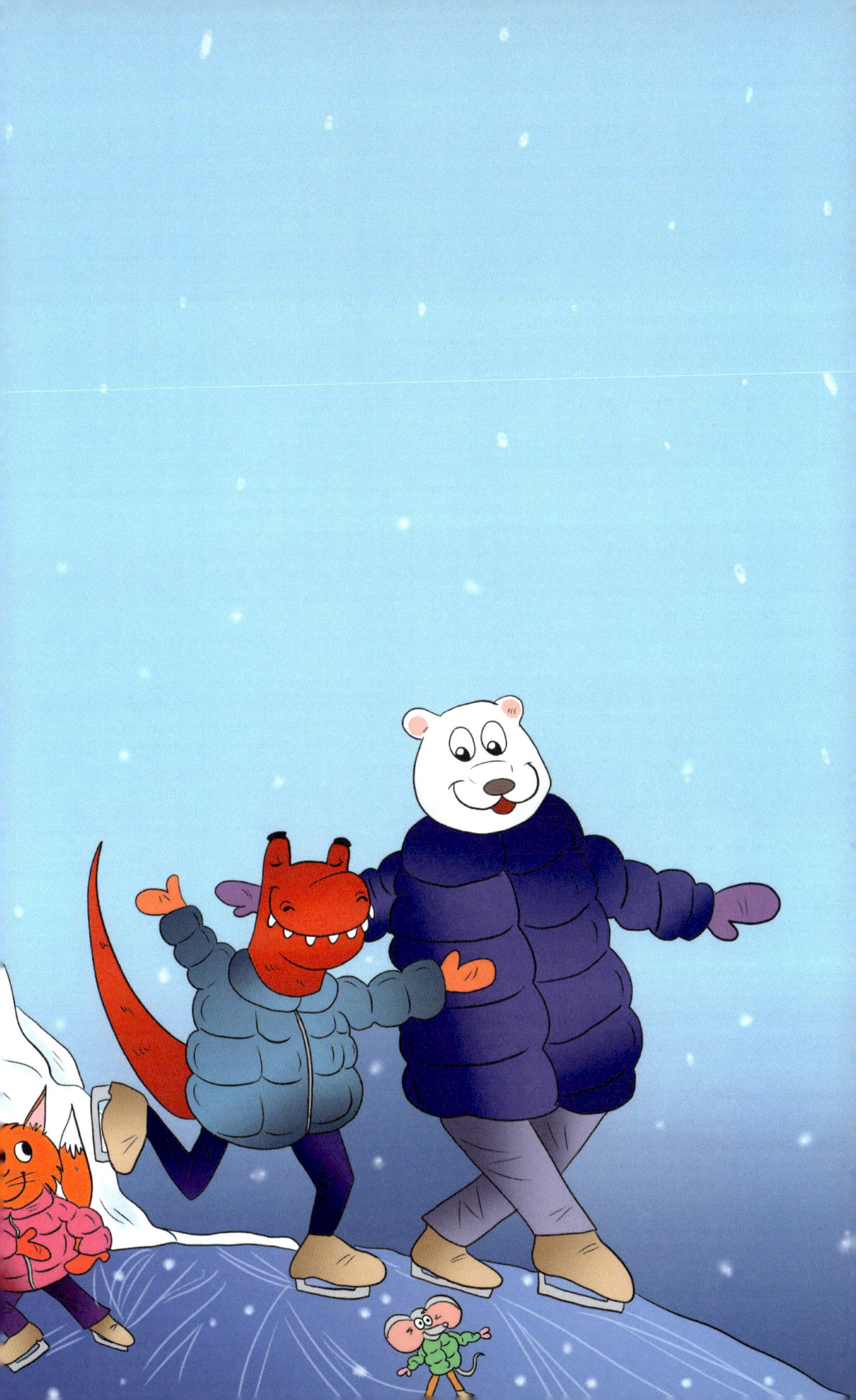

He sat
down with the
penguins
Ten to
twelve
at least
They ate
frosty cakes
and ice cream
A dinosaur
freezing
feast

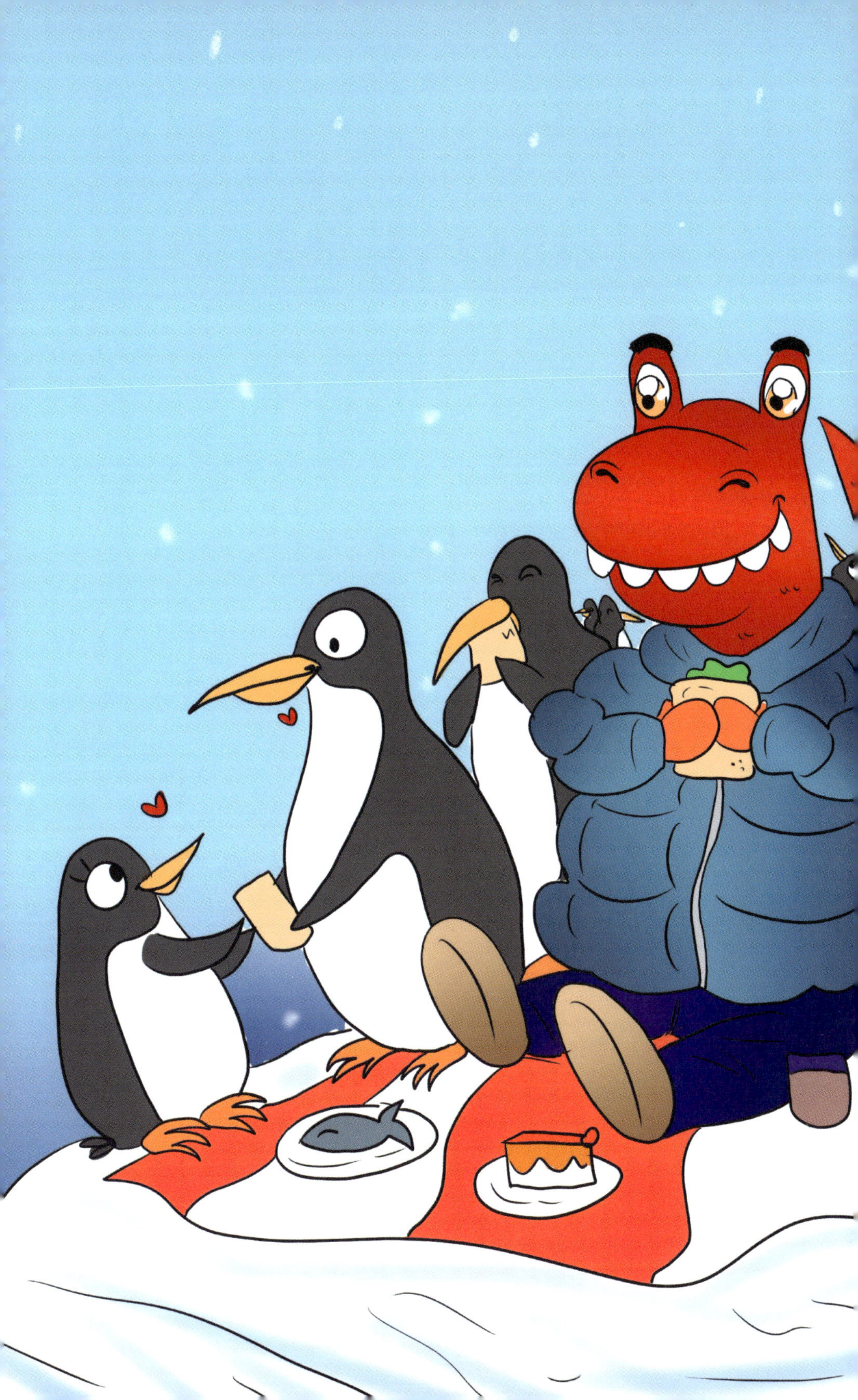

He flew
up to the
USA
And got
on a talk
show
The crowds
adored the
T-Rex
His support
began to
grow

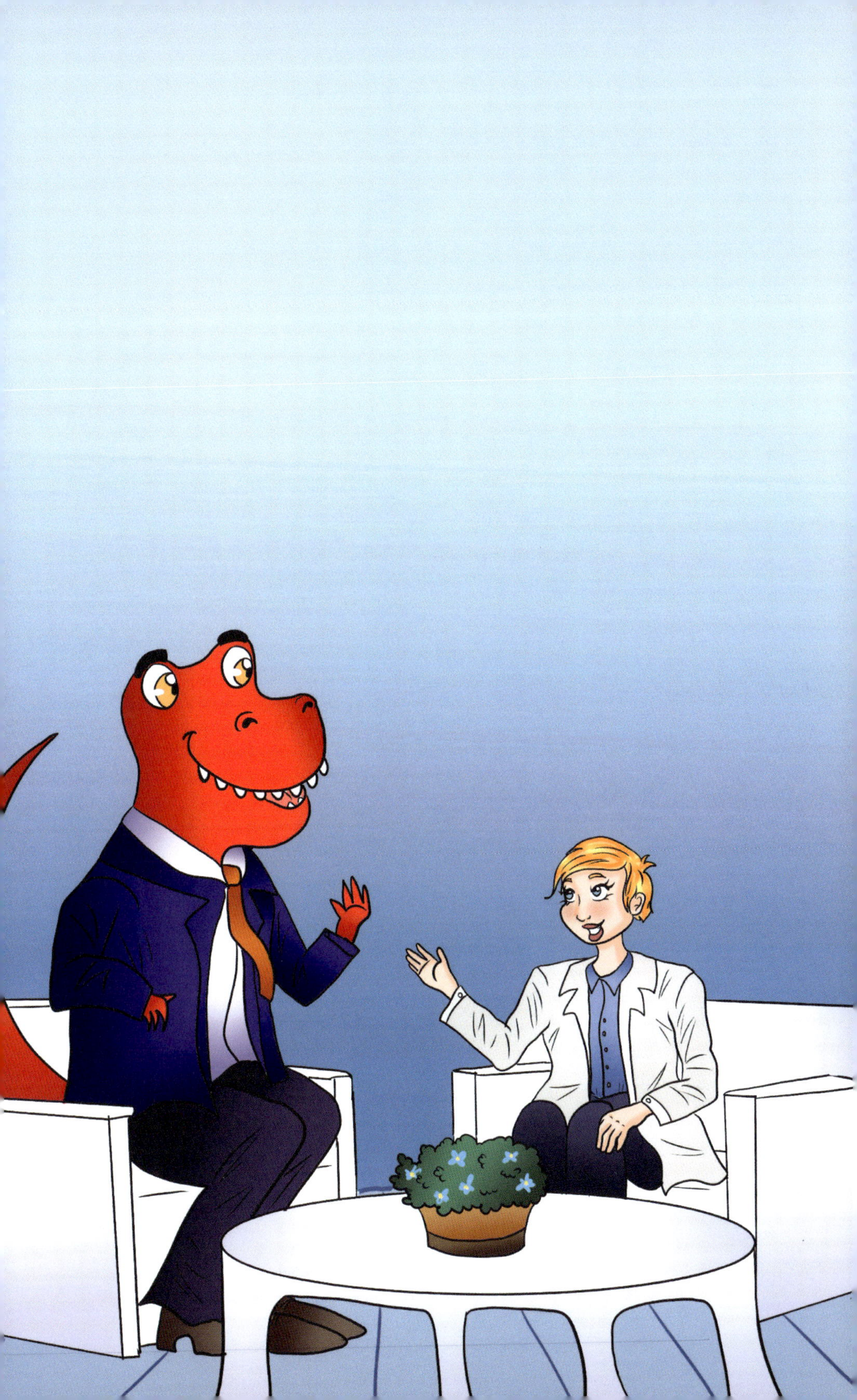

He decided
to run for
president
And went
on an election
tour
The people
voted
unanimously
For
President
Dinosaur

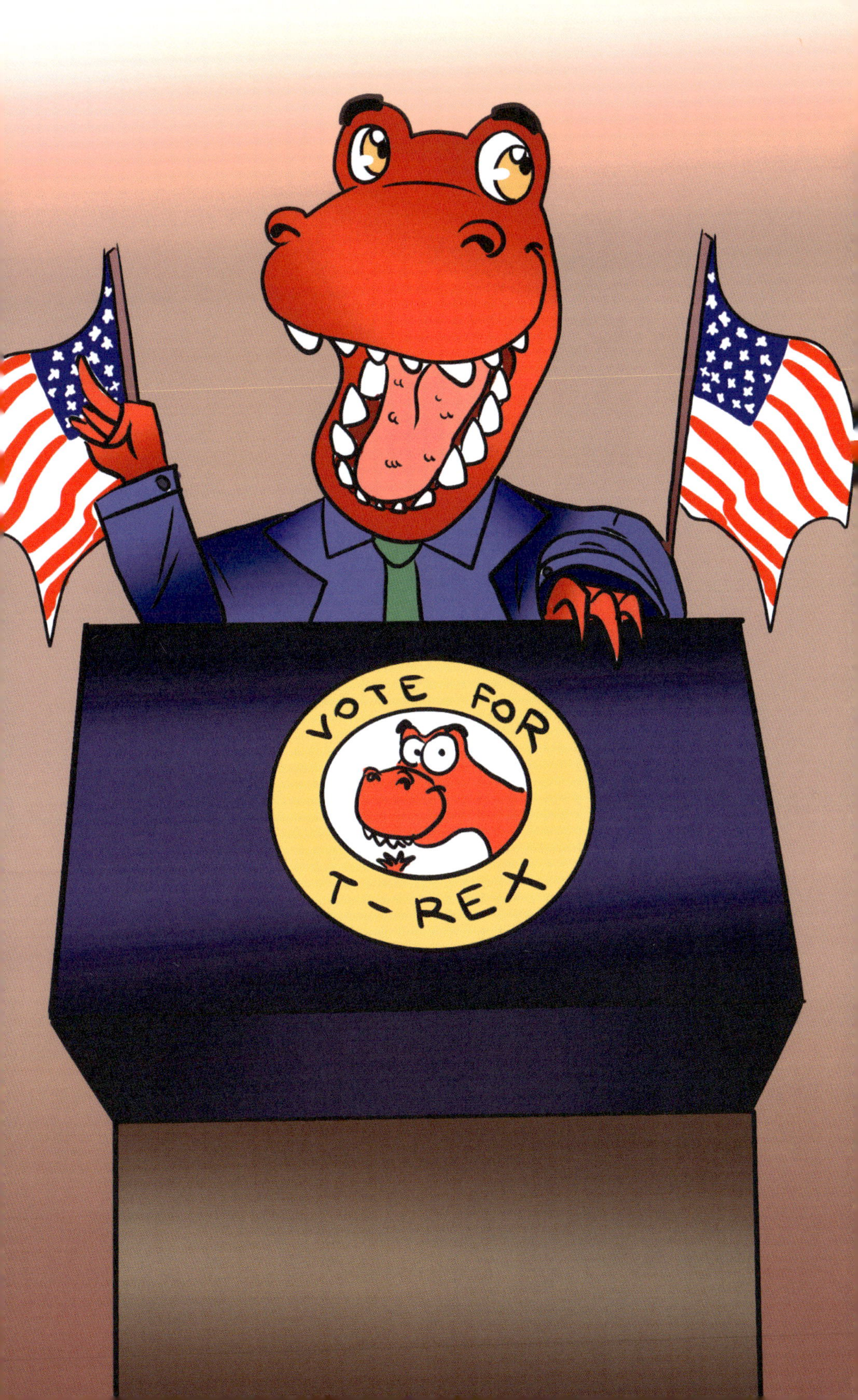
VOTE FOR
T-REX

He boarded
onto Air
Force One
And flew
down to
Brazil
He enjoyed
his travels
very much
But now
it was time
to chill

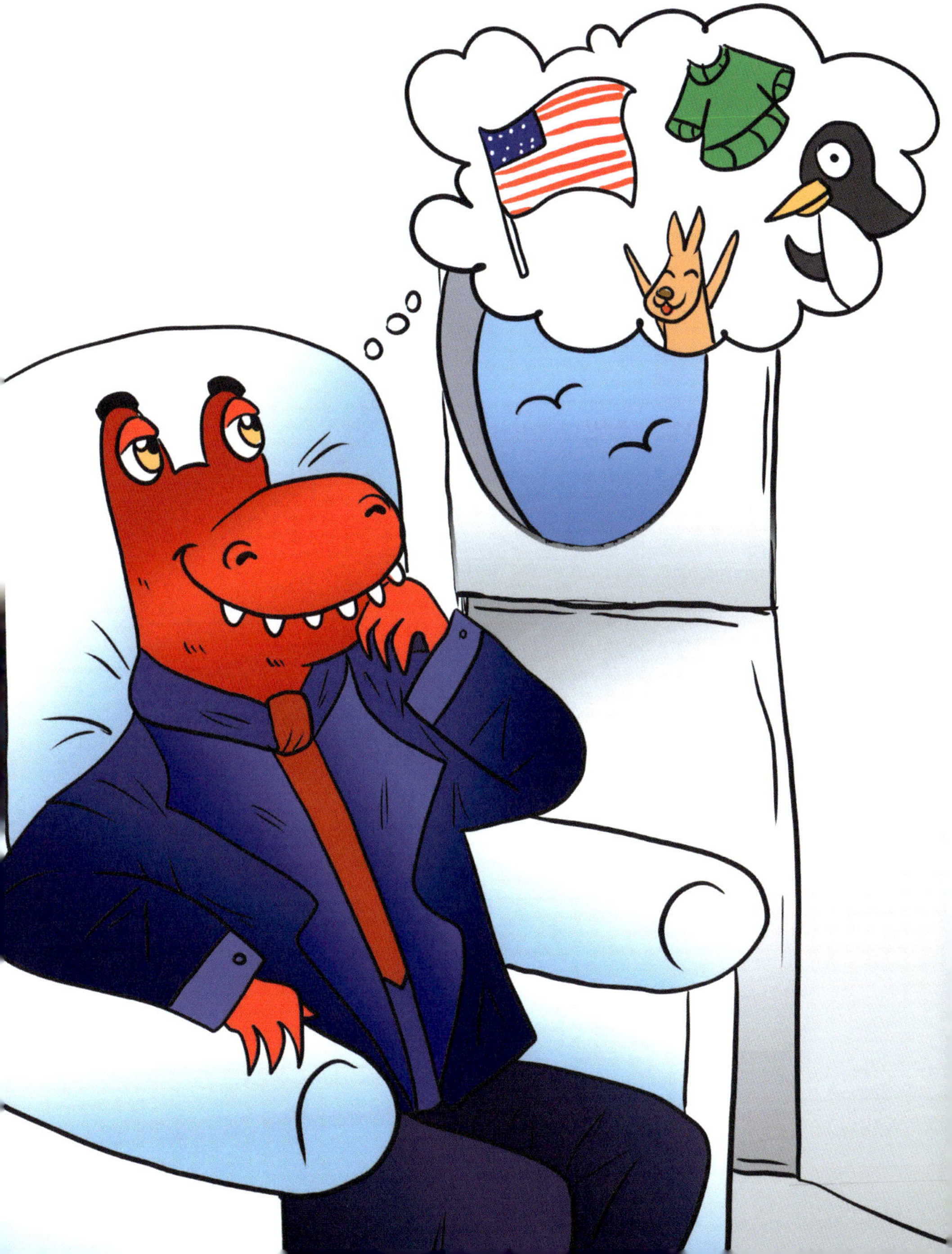

He went
   into the
         Amazon
To end
   his jet set
            tour
Because a
   dinosaur's
   favourite thing to do
   Is still to
   trample and roar

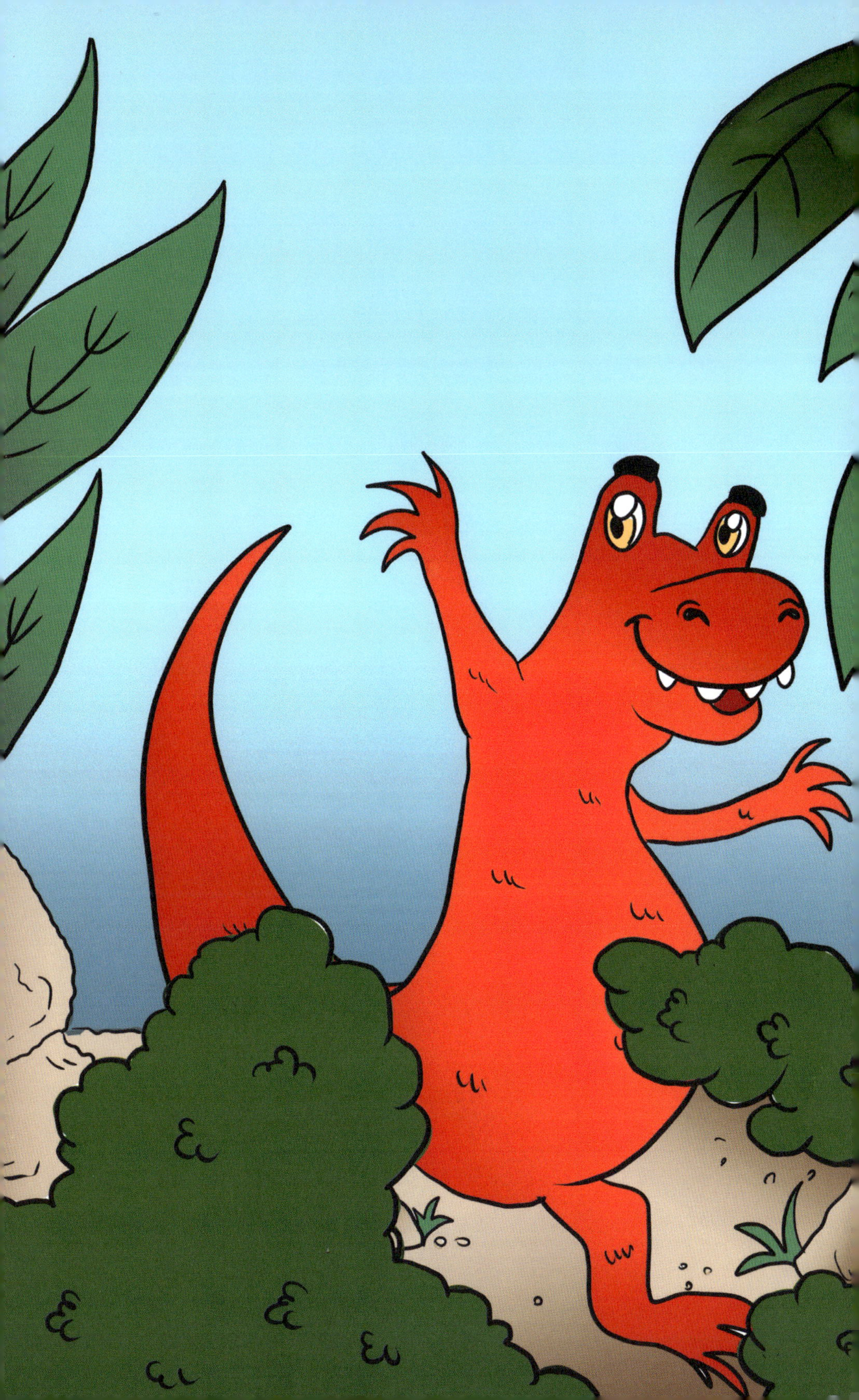

Want more **FREE BOOKS** by *Christopher Quirk.* Visit
www.thealexanderbooks.com

Printed in Great Britain
by Amazon